DORA'S EGGS

by Julie Sykes

illustrated by Jane Chapman

LITTLE TIGER PRESS
London

Dora was sitting on a nest of eggs.
They were shiny brown and smooth
to touch.
"These are my very first eggs,"
clucked Dora proudly.
"I must get all my friends to
come and admire them."

Dora climbed out of the hen house
and into the farmyard.
"Who shall I visit first?" she asked.
"I know! I'll go and find Doffy Duck."

Dora hopped over the fence and across the
field until she reached the pond.
"Hello, Doffy," called Dora. "Would you like to
come and see my eggs?"
"I can't come now," quacked Doffy. "I'm teaching
my babies to swim."

Dora stood watching the ducklings
splashing around and learning to paddle.
Somehow she felt a bit less excited.
"My eggs are nice," she thought.
"But those fluffy ducklings are
much nicer."

Dora felt just a little sad as she trotted
off to the sty to visit Penny Pig.
"Hello, Penny," she clucked. "Would you
like to come and see my eggs?"
But Penny didn't hear. She was having
too much fun, tumbling around with her
wriggly piglets.

Dora gave a little sigh.
"My eggs are nice," she said. "But
those wriggly piglets are much nicer."

Dora gave another little sigh as she climbed the hill to find Sally Sheep. "Would you like to come and see my eggs?" she asked Sally.

"Not today," bleated Sally. "I'm too busy keeping an eye on my lambs."

Dora looked at the lambs, frolicking in the field. She felt rather glum. "My eggs are nice," she thought. "But those playful lambs are much nicer."

Very sadly, Dora walked back to the farmyard.
On her way she bumped into Daisy Dog.
"Hello, Daisy," clucked Dora. "Would you like
to come and see my eggs?"
"Sorry, Dora," barked Daisy, wagging her tail.
"I can't come now. I'm taking my puppies
for a walk."

Dora was beginning to feel
quite miserable.
"My eggs are nice," she said.
"But those puppies out
for a walk are much nicer."

In the farmyard Dora stopped at the cowshed. She wished she felt happier, but perhaps Clarissa the Cow would cheer her up. "Would you like to see my eggs?" she called.

"Sssh," mooed Clarissa softly, nodding her head at the straw. Snuggled up by her feet and fast asleep was a newborn calf. Dora felt like crying. "My eggs are nice," she whispered. "But that little calf, all snuggled up, is much nicer."

Dora walked back across the yard in the sunlight and climbed into the hen house. Her eggs were just as she left them, smooth and brown and very still. "My eggs are nice," sighed Dora, fluffing out her feathers. "But everyone else's babies are *much* nicer."

Very sadly, Dora settled
herself down on to
her nest . . .

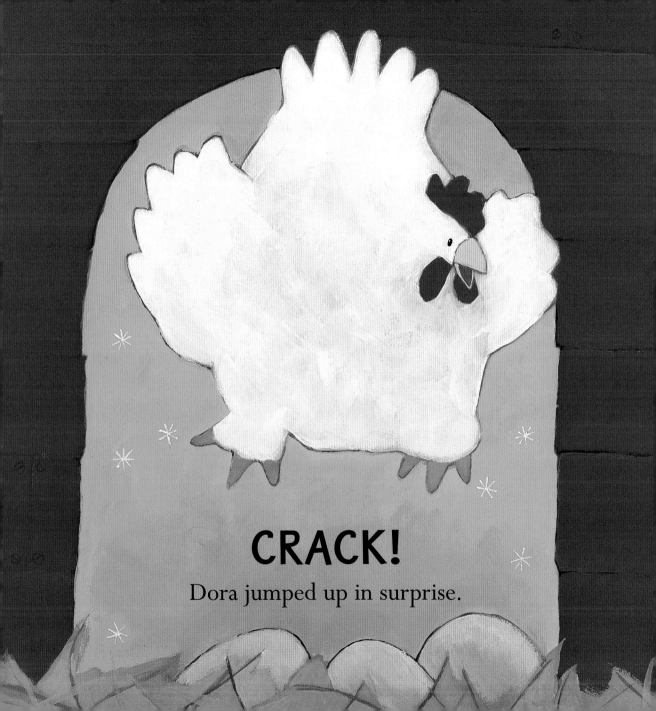

CRACK!

Dora jumped up in surprise.

"Oh no!" cried Dora. "I've broken them!"
Tears began to roll down her face.
They splashed on to the nest and over
the cracked eggs. As each tear fell,
the cracks grew wider and wider until
suddenly . . .

. . . up popped a fluffy head,
then another, and another.

Soon the nest was full of
tiny chicks.
"Cheep, cheep," the chicks
squeaked. "Cheep, cheep."
Dora stopped crying and
stared.

It didn't matter that the eggs were broken.
The new chicks were everything
Dora had ever wanted!
Proudly she strutted out into the farmyard,
and one by one the chicks followed after her.
All the animals stopped and stared.

"Why, Dora!" quacked Doffy.
"They're as fluffy as my ducklings!"
"And wriggly like my piglets,"
oinked Penny.
"They're as playful as my lambs,"
baaed Sally.
"And you can take them for walks —
just like my puppies," barked Daisy.
"But best of all," mooed Clarissa,
"your chicks can snuggle up to you,
like my calf snuggles up to me."
"Cluck," said Dora happily, agreeing
with her friends. "My eggs were
nice, but my chicks are much,
much nicer!"